BoJo's

Crapping on Britain since August 2019

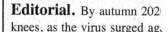

Editorial. By autumn 202⟨
knees, as the virus surged ag⟨
to pretend a 2nd lockdown wouldn't be needed,
and continued lining the pockets of their mates
instead of funding the people who actually knew
how to tackle the crisis. Only a PM who was
totally mad, remorselessly vindictive or utterly
clueless would go ahead and impose a super-hard
Brexit on a country already facing such troubles
… so things were certainly about to get worse!

We may despair at what is happening to our
country, but *Bojo's Woe Show* is here to help. It
won't bring down this dreadful government, but it
hopes to raise a smile, and maybe even a laugh,
and make these grim days for Britain just a little
bit happier. Since we have a clown show in
charge, it seems rude not to laugh at them.
Presented here are 65 original cartoons, lovingly
enhanced and expanded from the Twitter
versions. So sit back and enjoy the ride!

Thanks are due to Andrew Milne for some
beautiful London backdrop images, and to
everyone who retweets me on Twitter

DEDICATION:

If you've ever taken a stand against xenophobia,
corruption, dishonesty, rampant greed or anything
else Boris Johnson represents, even just by
voting, then this book is dedicated to you.

BoJo's Woe Show

Edition **106**

Crapping on Britain since August 2019

Catastrophus Copulatus

27th August 2020

| Tory chaos continues. | UK Media deny that they are easily distracted from important issues by dead cat stories about … what? What was that? Someone has quit *Strictly*? Hold the front page!!! |

BoJo's Woe Show

Edition **107**

Crapping on Britain since August 2019

Catastrophus Copulatus

26th August 2020

The BBC's Laura Kuenssberg interviews Johnson about his "achievements". | **Predictably, he gets an easy ride.**

Phwaff! So many great achieve-ments this year!! So many! Wehh weh which shall I talk about first?

Whichever you want, Prime Minister.

Right!!! Ah ah ah … yes. Lots of achievements. Phwaff!! Erm … phwoff!! Well, quite a lot of Brits aren't dead from the virus yet. That counts, right?

… and, ahhhhh, a baby! I had a baby and three months later I still know its name! Dear little Wilbur!!

Well you got Brexit done, didn't you, you hunky man.

Yes! Brilliant! I got Brexit done. All I had to do was agree a worse deal than the awful one I rejected, then pretend I didn't!

… and I made up a joke about briefs! How great am I?

Of course the real achievements were all by me. Delaying the Russia report. Redacting it. Herd immunity. Sticking the fat git in hospital for a month so people forgot how useless he was. Proving that I'm above the law.

Funnelling countless billions into my mates' bank accounts.

Moving forward, we intend to make the most of our respective talents, by which I mean I'll do all the actual ruining – I mean running – of the country while Boris will try to remember to put his underpants on before his trousers.

Ahh ah ah, yes, uhh, right, but er, what do I do with the rest of the day?

Well there are quite a few women walking around who aren't pregnant yet.

BoJo's Woe Show

Edition **108**

*Crapping on Britain
since August 2019*

Catastrophus *Copulatus*

29th August 2020

Having been utterly unconcerned about every other business wrecked by Covid or Brexit, the Tories find one they suddenly care about.

Johnson won't of course interrupt his holiday for anything other than a national emergency …

BoJo's Woe Show

Edition **109**

Crapping on Britain since August 2019

30th August 2020

Catastrophus   Copulatus

Sunak goes off script, briefly suggesting it might be a good idea to actually tax people who have more money than they need.

| **The idea is quickly forgotten, never to be heard again.**

Tax rises …

Taxing the rich, and the most profitable corporations…

Tell me Sunak, have you suddenly turned into *Jeremy Corbyn*?

W-w-we have to fill the hole in our finances somehow!

Have you forgotten which party you're in, Sunak? We get our money by taxing the poor, and taking away their benefits!

We're doing all that! We're doing all that!! And I've been enjoying it immensely! But it doesn't actually net us that much money, because the rich have already got it all –

– we've been in power ten years, remember! So we need to take a little from the rich as well, so we can …

So you can make yourself more popular? I think not. There will be **NO** taxing of the rich. Not one penny.

You will announce your resignation immediately, citing incurable narcissism as your reason.

As you wish. I'll leave you to watch this 2 day montage of speeches by Liz Truss, while you think it over.

I just want to be loved!

Never!

Aaaarrgghh! Noooooo!!!

New Pork Markets!

BoJo's Woe Show

Edition **110**

Crapping on Britain since August 2019

1st Sept 2020

Catastrophus   *Copulatus*

The BBC gets a new director, Tim Davie, a Tory who wants a "war on woke lefties."

Davie promptly cancels *The Mash Report*, because apparently poking fun at the government of the day is unacceptably left wing, in his view.

DOCTOR WHO

EXTERMINATE!

Eeek!

Zap!

Aaargh!

Zap!

Aiaieeee!!!

Doctor! We have to do something! The Daleks are killing everybody!!

Yes, Yaz. But a bit of extermination is also good for the economy. And it'll help discourage asylum seekers from coming here.

Let's leave them to it, and go spend money on some things that we don't really need.

Vworrp!

Vworrp!

What do you think, my masters?

Phwaff! You've certainly got rid of the woke-ness, Wormtim.

Well *I'm* not happy with the negative portrayal of the Daleks!

Can't we have an episode where the Daleks exterminate a load of people trying to cross the ocean, and then get cheered like heroes by the locals on the shore?

By your command

BoJo's Woe Show

Edition **111**

Crapping on Britain since August 2019

6th Sept 2020

Catastrophus   *Copulatus*

Desperate Brexitters want to replace a tiny fraction of the trade lost with the EU, via sovereignty-destroying trade deals.

The barrel is scraped very deeply indeed for candidates to go round the world making the deals …

Jimmy Saville? — Dead.

Kim Jong Un? — Busy.

Katie Hopkins? — Bankrupt and broken.

Laurence Fox? — Hates lefties too much.

I'm sorry … what?

I don't understand.

There's no such thing as 'too much'!

(sigh) … The person would need to be able to hide their loathing long enough to sign a trade deal.

Fox just isn't that good an actor.

I know! I know! What about Ian Botham? He used to be really good at hitting cricket balls … so … uhhh ….

I'm not going to dignify that with a reply.

Ideally it should be someone with a very limited attention span and grasp of English, so they don't notice all the rights we're signing away.

New loss of sovereignty markets!!

How about Prince Andrew? He's utterly incompetent, with no skills or abilities of any kind! He'll fit right in, around here!

We're going with Tony Abbott. Having a sexist, homophobic, talentless science-denying failed Prime Minister negotiating our trade deals ……

… wasn't working, so we'll try someone similar, but Australian.

BoJo's Woe Show

Edition 112

Crapping on Britain since August 2019

Catastrophus *Copulatus*

7th Sept 2020

The Sunday Times has another of those occasional moments where it notices how awful and useless Johnson is.

Persistent rumours abound that the pretty boy next door fancies the top job for himself.

Y-you have to DO something, Cummings!! Sob! Find some dirt on the bastard before he finishes me off!

THE SUNDAY TIMES
Second wave: 3000 new cases
Boris really isn't very good at

I knew I should have gone with Gove instead of you, you useless, lazy, steaming pile of horse crap!!

Could you try doing some work? Reading your notes? Preparing? We tried smearing Starmer, and it didn't work.

N-not him, you fool! SUNAK! He wants my job!

Yes, compared to you, Sunak does look competent, and almost kind. But then, so would a malfunctioning Dalek with rabies.

Oh, and if you ever call me a fool again, I will totally destroy you. Got it?

Still, the point is valid. We can't have Mr *I'm-so-pretty* moving in here, he might get illusions of actually being in charge. Time for a bit of Brexit level chaos to come his way, I think …

... courtesy of a little reshuffle at the Treasury.

We're your new deputies! Grayling's the name!

And I've got some great *mutant algorithms* the boss told me to try out!

BoJo's Woe Show

Edition 113

Crapping on Britain since August 2019

Catastrophus Copulatus

7th Sept 2020

Johnson promised voters an oven-ready Brexit deal, in perhaps the most blatant lie in UK electoral history.

9 months later, there still isn't a deal, and Johnson increasingly tries to engineer a No-Deal to hide this reality.

You promised voters an oven-ready Brexit deal. Why are you now aiming for No Deal?

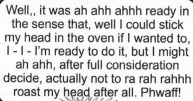

Well,, it was ah ahh ahhh ready in the sense that, well I could stick my head in the oven if I wanted to, I - I - I'm ready to do it, but I might ah ahh, after full consideration decide, actually not to ra rah rahhh roast my head after all. Phwaff!

So what you're saying is, you sold the public a deal that you never intended to honour?

Did I say that? I don't think I said that. I'm not really sure what I said. But no Deal will be Great for Britain! Yes!

Even when all the available evidence shows it'll be a disaster?

Evidence? Ahhh, I don't really care about that … after all, thehh thehh they said all the evidence showed that I'd be a terrible Prime Minister … and … err … all the evidence since then … err…. you can't trust evidence, basically. Phwaff!!

Wer wer what matters is fer feh feh freedom to choose, complete independence and no more external control!

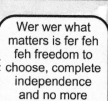

… because once I've delivered No Deal, Cummings has said he might quit, and let me start making some of my own decisions.

BoJo's Woe Show

Edition **114**

Crapping on Britain since August 2019

8th Sept 2020

Catastrophus Copulatus

Throughout the pandemic, Johnson and his underlings awarded contracts worth colossal amounts to people whose only qualification was a close relationship with someone in the party, and/or being a big donor to party funds.

We're going to, ah ahh ahhh … commit 100 million pounds to fighting the virus! Phwaff!!

Don't spend it all at once! Phwaff!!

£££

Uhh, we probably should know what he's spending it on, so we can lie about it properly

I suppose we should ask.

Drugs, parties, weapons deals, my retirement fund, and propping up facist dictators, here and there.

Trump's short of cash, apparently.

And I'll give a bit to Alan Sugar, too.

He begged.

Suppose I'll throw in a few second hand gowns for nurses too, just to show willing.

Well that all seems perfectly in order. Phwaff!! Bye bye Covid, hello re-election!

Johnson you complete and utter braindead excuse for a moron!!! That guy *WASN'T* one of our Brexit backers!!!

Oh!

Today we are committing *another* 100 million pounds to the fight against coronavirus.

BoJo's Woe Show

Edition **115**

*Crapping on Britain
since August 2019*

Catastrophus   *Copulatus*

9th Sept 2020

Things Tories aren't good at: running the country, helping people (other than the super-rich), honesty, handling pandemics, protecting wildlife. | **Things Tories *are* good at: finding other people to blame for their failures.**

V-virus cases keep going up! They'll say it's my fault!

Phwaff! Don't worry, we'll just blame it all on young people. They never vote for us anyway.

The predicted job losses from your planned No Deal Brexit look absolutely horrendous!!

Bwahhh … all the EU's fault! Phwaff!! And the remainers'. Nothing to do with us.

Uhhh, boss, lots of Special Needs kids are missing out on school, apparently! I saw it on the telly last night.

Labour's fault! Somehow.

One of our big Brexit donors is angry! They haven't been given a Covid contract, and they're not happy.

Phwahh! We've already got their money, so I don't phwacking care. It's their own fault for expecting me to keep my word.

That donor happens to be a **personal friend** of mine, you floundering sack of pig's vomit! There are some promises you *DO* need to keep, you useless turd!

Hancock!!! How *dare* you fail to give Dom's friend a contract! Give him a billion pounds, right away! Take it out of nurses' pay.

Y-yes sir.

BoJo's Woe Show

Edition **116**

Crapping on Britain since August 2019

10th Sept 2020

Catastrophus  *Copulatus*

Johnson has a closed door meeting with Tory MPs.	His line seems to be that his own withdrawal agreement, which he had promoted as "oven ready" in order to win the election, has nothing to do with him.

I don't know who wrote this stupid, **stupid** withdrawal agreement, but it's all **your** fault for voting for it!

I know! I know who wrote it! It was …

He said we **don't know**, you moron!

But we **do** know! It was y-*mmmmfff!!*

We **don't know** who wrote it.

But you said the deal was "*oven ready*" and -

No questions!!!

We don't want to go back to the dark days of last autumn, with MPs expressing opinions, and losing the whip for … for … I can't remember what for …

For not backing this deal, wasn't it?

SHUT UP!!!

You need to look at it from my point of view, because yours … well, yours doesn't matter. This isn't the Lib Dems!!

But don't worry, we're just going to break a few international laws, and that should fix it all. Phwaff!!

But isn't breaking the law, uhhh, kinda … bad?

I said no questions!!!

What do you think this is – a democracy???

BoJo's Woe Show

Edition **117**

Crapping on Britain since August 2019

Catastrophus Copulatus

14th Sept 2020

Johnson is utterly demolished by Ed Miliband during a commons debate.

His response is to slouch on the bench like a drunken tramp and say nothing.

What incompetence! What failure of governance!! This is his deal, his mess, his failure.

Either he wasn't straight with the country, or he didn't understand it. Or both.

He didn't read the protocol, he hasn't read the bill, **he doesn't know his stuff!!!**

This is awful!!! But as long as Boris doesn't speak, we might still win the vote.

He won't.

I locked the brainless fat pig in a cupboard, and put a dummy on his bench.

So far, no-one has noticed!

That's odd. The dummy just stamped its foot.

Dom! DOM!

I just found the PM locked in a cupboard!

He was tied up and gagged with a sign saying "*do not untie under any circumstances*"!

So you left him there. Please tell me you left him there …

No I freed him! How'd he do the debate, otherwise?

Why am I surrounded by **complete and utter morons**???

Don't ask us, you picked the Cabinet!

Ehhh bweh bwehh Winston Churchil

Stop worrying. Tory MPs would vote to legalise baby eating if we told them to.

BoJo's Woe Show

Edition **118**

Crapping on Britain since August 2019

8th Sept 2020

Catastrophus   Copulatus

Testing centres run out of virus test kits.	The Tory response is to pretend it isn't happening, and distract the public with lots of "tough on crime" pronouncements*.	*Crimes by other people, that is.

There's no virus tests left, anywhere in Britain! None at all!! Some idiot forgot to check if we had enough!!!

Ooer!! I'm on the telly later! What'll I say?

Just *lie through your teeth*, you idiots! Haven't I taught you *anything*?

There are plenty of tests, don't worry…

No there aren't! I've been to TEN testing centres today, and not **one** had a single test!

Well … errr… that just shows how successful we've been in gettin' people to have virus tests!

No, there hasn't been a single test delivered to this centre, this month!

Oh … errr … errr …

Lie through your teeth, lie through your teeth!

Actually, we're bringin' in **new** tests.

Anyone with virus-like symptoms will be tested on English language and history. If they sound a bit foreign, or can't name all the monarchs in order, then we'll deport them.

That'll soon bring down the infection rate, here!

Dunno how she guessed our plan, but now she's *told* them, they won't go!

That's the idea, you pillock! If they're all too scared to get tested, then we can pretend there are no new cases!

BoJo's Woe Show

Edition **119**

Crapping on Britain since August 2019

16th Sept 2020

David Cameron surfaces, probably concerned about book sales, to very weakly criticize Johnson's (specific and limited) law-breaking Brexit approach.

Major, Blair, Brown and even May are all far more strident in their criticisms.

What **all** of them? Even *Theresa May*?

Yes, Sir.

Well I don't want to be left out. People might start to think I'm irrelevant.

Quite.

Perhaps I should give a talk about the dangers of making foolhardy decisions (two grand a ticket). But it's not something I know much about. What should I say, Butkins?

Perhaps Sir might use the term "misgivings."

Very non-committal. I like it.

Every living PM is against us! Even pigboy! It'll make people think we're getting it wrong!

Worry not, my friends! *Cura non*! I have made contact with one who might be more … supportive …

What have you done to my party, you blundering imbeciles??

Ooer!

You're bankrupting Britain and destroying our reputation, all to make a few billion-aires richer, who aren't even British!

Having come up with a such a paralyzingly stupid idea, you couldn't even deliver it properly! How dare you make MY party look so painfully inept? How DARE you?

When you die, I'll punish you all!!!

Uhh, Dom, I think you'll have to think of a different plan.

L-later. I need to drive to Barnard Castle to buy some clean underpants.

BoJo's Woe Show

Edition **120**

Crapping on Britain since August 2019

Catastrophus   Copulatus

17th Sept 2020

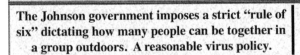

| The Johnson government imposes a strict "rule of six" dictating how many people can be together in a group outdoors. A reasonable virus policy. | But there's an exemption for posh people who want to go around slaughtering wildlife. |

SEVEN PEOPLE! I see **seven** of you together! *POLICE*!! *You're all goin' to jail!!!*

But we're on *your* side!

The woke brigade got too much power! No-one's allowed to have *any* other views! It says so in the Sun, the Mail, and the Express!

KILL THE MUZLIMS

FORRIN OUT

BRITTIN FIRST

You read **three** papers? Wot are you, a fookin' intellectewal?

I mostly look at the pictures

Well it's true, of course. The left controls *everything* in this country. Oh dear, I'm really conflicted, now …

They are plebs, Patel. *Homo inferius sunt.* Unless they can demonstrate a 6 figure weekly income, or descent from the nobility, they should all be sent to the workhouse.

Phwaff!! I think we can, ah ahhh ahhh, find a way to place these fine gentlemen *outside* of the rule of six …

Cheers, mate!

Wot's a grouse?

Can we shoot some asylum seekers, too?

BoJo's Woe Show

Edition **121**

Crapping on Britain since August 2019

17th Sept 2020

Catastrophus *Copulatus*

Covid test shortage continues, making it hard to contain the virus, and the public rightly complain.

Rees Mogg tells them to stop "carping on" about it.

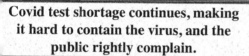

Plebs should stop **carping on** about not getting Covid tests.

Homines non-importantium cessandum Cyprinus-carpio.

If I had my way, they'd be too busy worrying about rickets, scurvy and consumption, to care about Covid.

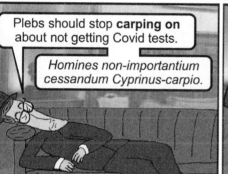

Poor people have no business living to age 40, let alone 80.

They should be celebrating the fact that pupils at Eton get tested twice a day, and can now go grouse shooting with all their servants.

If a person wants a covid test, all they need do is donate a few million pounds to party funds, and then they can run their own test and trace service. So no more carping, please.

I've just got your test results back, Mr Mogg. You don't have it

Really? Are you sure?

The test was very conclusive, sir. You have no soul at all.

Oh.

BoJo's Woe Show

Edition **122**

Crapping on Britain since August 2019

Catastrophus Copulatus

18th Sept 2020

Biden says no US trade deal if Johnson breaks the Good Friday agreements. Tories and their lackeys decry this as "foreign interference."

Which is like accusing someone of interfering with your life, if they refuse to go out with you.

Uhh, boss, Joe Biden says there'll be no US trade deal, if we break the GFA!

What's it got to do with him?

Well he might be president next year.

Shut up, you absolute phwacking *imbecile*!!! I don't care if he's going to be Lord President of the phwacking Galaxy!!! He still doesn't get to decide which promises we break!

Dom!! Help me stamp out all this *foreign interference*!

Mr Putin? I hate to ask, but could you up your efforts to get Donald re-elected? We'll channel some more money your way, of course.

New bortscht markets!

I'm afraid the EU's saying the same thing, too. No GFA, no trade deal.

What???

This is unacceptable! **WE** get to decide who we do trade deals with!! No-one else. If *they* broke their word, we'd say "*no deal with you*" – and quite right, too!

Why do all these foreigners keep interfering!!

There is indeed far too much foreign influence in British affairs. Mr Smith, you will write a strongly worded article denouncing it.

Yes Mr Murdoch, right away Mr Murdoch, sir!

BoJo's Woe Show

Edition **123**

*Crapping on Britain
since August 2019*

Catastrophus — *Copulatus*

21st Sept 2020

Major crisis revealed, which dwarfs Brexit and the pandemic: Boris Johnson has to struggle through life on only 150K a year, and cannot even afford a nanny!!

Gove is well known to be after the top spot for himself.

I can't do it! I can't survive on 150K a year! Oh poor, poor me!!

Eh? You said you were earning 3000 pounds an hour!

He is. He only works an hour a week.

Yes but I'm not paid by the *hour*, am I? If I was, I'd work 2 hours a week, and double my salary!!

I could just about scrape by on 300K.

Easily solved! Let's swap jobs!

This could work in our favour. The plebs are always carping on about not being able to afford food, or clothing.

Now that Boris is *even poorer than they are*, we won't seem so out of touch.

Good point! Get onto the tabloids and tell them how poor poor Boris is!

What's going on?? Gove!!! *Why would they do this to me!*

No idea. I don't know anyone who works for them.

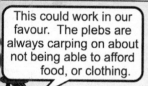
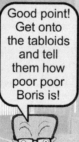

Daily ✠ Mail

EXCLUSIVE: WE KNEW BORIS WAS A BAD 'UN ALL ALONG!

BORIS: What a useless **!**

And they're saying our virus messaging isn't clear. It's **perfectly** clear!! If you're poor you follow the rules, if you're rich you do what you like! Same as with everything else!!

Why can't they understand that?? It's simple!!!

I know! Why not Hop on a private jet to Italy and go to some Bunga-Bunga parties with Russian billionaires. That'll certainly make all the plebs start liking you, again. Definitely.

Thanks, Govey. Thank God I've got a friend like you.

BoJo's Woe Show

Edition **124**

*Crapping on Britain
since August 2019*

Catastrophus *Copulatus*

24th Sept 2020

Massive hold-ups and truck queues are (correctly) predicted for Kent as a hard Brexit approaches. The suggested solution is a border around Kent.	Honestly, I am not making this up. The Tories really did suggest this.

Phwaff!! Now they're saying there'll be queues of 7000 lorries in Kent! Bloody remoaners and their worst case scenarios!

Actually that's *our* prediction. And it's our **best** case scenario. But it's OK, they won't blame ME.

All those foreign truck drivers stuck in queues without food, water or toilets for days! *Oooh!* I'm gettin horny just *thinkin'* about it!

But the chaos will hurt the **economy!**

I know! I know!! Let's just put border posts for trucks all around Kent!

For ****'s sake Williamson!! Even by *your* standards, that's a bloody stupid idea!!

New breaking up the UK markets!!

Dom will have a better idea, won't you, Dom?

Border round Kent it is, then

I'll make the arrange-ments.

Wait a minute, wait a minute … won't that just lead to queues of 7000 trucks to get into Kent, instead?

Oh.

For goodness' sake, you two. We'll just put borders around Surrey and Sussex as well. Problem solved.

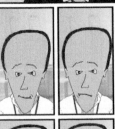

BoJo's Woe Show

Edition **125**

Crapping on Britain since August 2019

Catastrophus · *Copulatus*

24th Sept 2020

Two far-right news channels are planned for the UK, the now infamous GB News, and a British Fox News from Rupert Murdoch.

Meanwhile Laurence Fox's attention seeking, very public mid-life crisis continues.

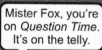

BoJo's Woe Show

Edition **126**

Crapping on Britain since August 2019

30th Sept 2020

Catastrophus *Copulatus*

| Johnson puts in places rules for everyone to follow regarding the virus. He then makes a total mess of explaining them on air. | Rumours of a rift between Sunak and Hancock over virus control measures. |

Phwaff!! In the Northeast, can meet up indoors, or maybe outdoors, in groups of more than 6. Or is it less than 6?

Ahh ahhh might have misspoke there. I think it's that you're not allowed. Anyway, hope that's all clear now.

Oh dear God!

And lots of **total nutters** are protesting about the new virus control measures!!

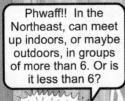

That's no way to speak about our backbench MPs!

Though you've got a point with Dorries.

No! I mean all the anti-maskers in Trafalgar square, spreading the virus! We need to *do* something!

How about a track and trace system that actually works?

Let's just send everyone back to work, and blame the public when they all start dying!

Piss off!

But that'll make me look incompetent!

LOOK incompetent?

Hey, YOU were the moron behind "*Eat out to spread it about*"

Mercenary *****!!

BIFF!

BASH! THUMP!!

Incompetent !!

What about the backbench rebels?

I'll have Boris speak to them. By the time he's done, they'll have no idea what it is they're objecting to.

BoJo's Woe Show

Edition **127**

*Crapping on Britain
since August 2019*

30th Sept 2020

Catastrophus — *Copulatus*

Johnson's latest excuse for not answering questions is to label all questioning of him as "unpatriotic", even at PMQs.

UK boss Dominic Cummings mysteriously disappears from view for many days.

BoJo's Woe Show

Edition **128**

*Crapping on Britain
since August 2019*

2nd Oct 2020

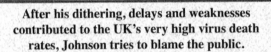

Catastrophus *Copulatus*

After his dithering, delays and weaknesses contributed to the UK's very high virus death rates, Johnson tries to blame the public.

Patel expresses desire to forcibly house migrants on sites outside the UK.

It's all your fault the virus is back! YOU – the public! YOU got complacent.

All you morons who broke the lockdown or didn't wear a mask in shops … err … hi, Dom, hi Dad.

… and all that eating out in restaurants just because some idiot told you to!

Someone gag him!!

None of this helps!!

Why can't we just load them all onto some broken down cruise liners, and ship them off to a remote prison island?

New porridge markets!

I hate asylum seekers as much as you, Patel, but we're in enough hot water over breaking international law as it is!

Actually I was talking about doing that to virus patients, but I like *your* idea better!

It's just too expensive to send asylum seekers or virus patients off to St Helena, I'm afraid. Good idea otherwise. Still, there might still be a way to use this idea to our benefit …

Phwaff!! Where did you say this boat was going?

BoJo's Woe Show

Edition **129**

Crapping on Britain since August 2019

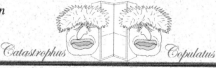

Catastrophus *Copulatus*

3rd Oct 2020

All parties hold virtual conferences due to Covid situation. | **Tory conference is plagued by IT problems …**

I am now going to list for you all the benefits of Brexit …

Oh no!! The entire IT system for our party conference just went down!

That means no-one can watch Gove!

Dammit!! I wanted them all to *suffer*!!

Uh, why? They're *our* people!

I just *like* suffering, **OK**?

How's it all going, Stupidly?

It's not. The entire system has crashed.

Nonsense! Chap I put in charge said he was an expert! Phwaff!! What was his name now? Gray … Gray something ...

Computer was getting a bit hot, so I poured water on it. Seems to have sorted it!

Oh well I'm sure it'll be fixed in time for the talk on computerised Brexit border checks …

I wonder how Gove's getting on?

Umm … err … I'm sure I'll think of one in a minute …

BoJo's Woe Show

Edition **130**

Crapping on Britain since August 2019

Catastrophus   *Copulatus*

5th Oct 2020

Priti Patel does her Tory conference speech.

Dalmatian puppies and asylum seekers run for cover.

… and the Kraken shall rise from the depths and consume all who attempt to cross the water!!!

Phwaff!! It's a nice idea, Patel, but I'm not sure we have the budget to build a giant refugee-eating sea monster.

Spoilsport!! And you were the one who said I couldn't just shoot and bomb them all.

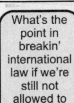

What's the point in breakin' international law if we're still not allowed to have *fun*?

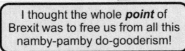

I thought the whole *point* of Brexit was to free us from all this namby-pamby do-gooderism!

So did I, but apparently slaughtering defenceless refugees is regarded as inhuman, for some reason.

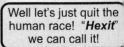

Well let's just quit the human race! "*Hexit*" we can call it!

Hmm. It might get in the way of us doing trade deals.

You'll have to content your-self with sending refugees to your new concentration camp in Antarctica, and not giving them any warm clothing.

Can I send EU citizens too? Can I? Can I??

All right. Since you asked nicely. But wait till the registration system crashes again, so they can't complain.

…and that, Tory members, is how I will make Britain a fairer country for everyone.

BoJo's Woe Show

Edition **131**

Crapping on Britain since August 2019

Catastrophus Copulatus

5th Oct 2020

"Catastrophic data error" sees 50000 people lost from contact tracing system after apparently having slipped off the end of a spreadsheet.

Sunak gives his Tory conference speech.

BoJo's Woe Show

Edition **132**

*Crapping on Britain
since August 2019*

Catastrophus   *Copulatus*

6th Oct 2020

Britain's worst ever Prime Minister addresses the Tory party conference.	Dorries seen apparently drunk in commons.	In a later speech, Johnson waffles about tooting bugles.

Phwaff!! Some people are saying that I'm incompetent! But let me tell you, I dehh deh don't even know the *meaning* of that word!

#CPC2020

Seriously, I don't. Dom, could you look it up for me? Thanks.

Anyway! Wehhh wehh wehh we can hear the **toot** of good news coming out of the **bugle** of my ... err ... toot toot!! It's good news!! ... yes! About ... errrr ...

... about . ..um ...how the news is **good**! Yes! *Well done to us!*

And I have a **vision** where there'll be no more bad news!! Because we're going to ban it. Only good news about the government will be allowed!

And good 'mews', too, if you have a well-behaved kitten, ha-ha.

Uhhh, Dom, no-ones laughing at my jokes. Where are all the sycophants?

The audience is all online, you fat moron!

Sho that's why I couldn't get sherved at the bar! Hic!

Yes Dorries, it probably was.

Phwaff!! Where was I? Oh yes. **Good news** – quite a few people have managed not to die after we totally failed to control the virus, and there are at least two countries with worse death rates than us ... errr...

Blue passports, everyone! Blue passports!!

BoJo's Woe Show

Edition **133**

*Crapping on Britain
since August 2019*

7th Oct 2020

Catastrophus   *Copulatus*

Tories increasingly rely on stoking culture wars as a means of feeding their base and distracting from their corruption and incompetence.

Their latest target? Good people. Or "do-gooders" as they call them.

Jesus Christ!

What is it, Patel?

Well they say He might rise again one day. So Jesus should go on the list, too.

Phwaff!! Good point.

So we've got Christ, Attenborough, Chris Packham, Captain Tom Moore, all the pro-EU lot, Judi Dench (lots of charity work, apparently), Bono, Bob Geldof, Prince Charles, Marcus Rashford …

Caroline Lucas. All the bloody Greens, in fact.

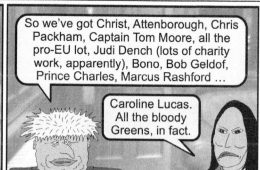

Come on, there must be some other do-gooders we can find to send to my concentration camps?

I know! I know! The Queen!! She's always doing good things

And she does always look at me with that strange expression, the same way she's started to look at Prince Andrew.

Oh. Maybe not, then.

With her gone, we'd have a president instead. So while I was doing that, someone else would have to babysit Boris.

Rishi Sunak!! Put him on the list!

Yeah, but the bastard's after my job.

What?? But he's one of us.

He must have done *something* good, maybe when he was a kid. We'll get him on that.

Nope. I can't find a single decent thing he's ever done.

Come on Patel!! What do I pay you for??

BoJo's Woe Show

Edition **134**

*Crapping on Britain
since August 2019*

Catastrophus   Copulatus

8th Oct 2020

With apologies to *Father Ted*

Johnson nominates Brexit enthusiast, "disgraced former defence secretary" Liam Fox for job as head of WTO. Fox is quickly eliminated from the process.

Tory MP Kawzcyntski appoint trade envoy for Mongolia.

Bad news, Bodge. They didn't want me at the WTO!

What? Why?!?

They said I was incompetent, self-interested and utterly divorced from reality!

Well we know your good points, but did they say why they rejected you?

Phwaff!! Never mind, we shall grasp the horn of international trade by the balls of …errm… err … you get the idea.

Kawzcyntski! You're our new Outer Mongolia trade envoy!! That'll show those WTO bastards!

Uhh thanks. Great honour. Hmmph.

New yak markets!

Ah, Truss, just the man. You can do the rest of our trade deals, all over the world.

New holiday markets!

Do you not think that her extremely limited vocabulary might pose a little problem there?

What? Why?

So I'll just sort it out, like I do everything else, then, shall I?

"Please!"

"Please!"

"Please!"

"*Please!*"

New!

P … p… new!

Pleeeeeyew!

New please markets!

Please can we have a trade deal?

Sigh … this is hopeless. I'll just give you a load of photocopies of our EU trade deal for them to sign, and hope no-one notices.

New world-beating incompetence markets!

BoJo's Woe Show

Edition **135**

Crapping on Britain since August 2019

9th Oct 2020

Catastrophus *Copulatus*

| No. 10 (i.e. Cummings) decides to appoint spokesperson to spout Tory propaganda, like Kelly Anne Conway did for Trump. | Allegra Stratton gets the job, despite Laura Kuenssberg having been doing it free for over a year. |

I've decided to hire someone to communicate with the public on your behalf, you useless fat oaf.

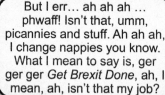

But I err… ah ah ah … phwaff! Isn't that, umm, picannies and stuff. Ah ah ah, I change nappies you know. What I mean to say is, ger ger ger *Get Brexit Done*, ah, I mean, ah, isn't that my job?

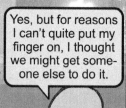

Yes, but for reasons I can't quite put my finger on, I thought we might get someone else to do it.

The virus will all be gone by Xmas, you'll be pleased to know.

Because despite all the money we've spaffed up the wall so far, I'm totally confident that Dom's mate Steve will have a world-beating track and trace scheme in place by Tuesday. And it's only costing you 30 billion pounds!

"Phwaff."

You're a sexy filly, aren't you! Woof! Fancy a quickie in the cabinet room? Not sure I've boffed anyone called Allegra before!

Cummings, you fool! You let *Boris* write it **himself**? He's just dropped 5 points in the "best PM" poll!

No! I gave her *my* script!

Someone must have switched them!

But who??

BoJo's Woe Show

Edition **136**

Crapping on Britain since August 2019

12th Oct 2020

Catastrophus *Copulatus*

Hancock makes a crass joke about the government's pandemic handling while breaking his own rules in the commons bar.

Government launches *"rethink, reskill, reboot"* campaign suggesting ballet dancers should work in cyber.

I say I say I say!!! What do you get when you cross Dominic Cummings with a track and trace system?

60000 dead people! Ha-hah! Ha-hah! Hahh!

No, but seriously, none of us would **ever** dare cross Dominic Cummings!

My God!! What's he doing??

New cringe markets!

Rethink, reskill, reboot! We'll all be for the chop once the backbench zombies finally wake up and ditch Fatty No-Brain, so we've been letting the website pick us new jobs. Hancock got comedian, for some reason.

I just got "c**t".

I got Prime Minister.

Liar!

When I tried it, the computer just made a sort of weeping noise, and crashed.

Oh, I'm glad it wasn't only me.

It said I should be making fur coats out of dalmatian puppies.

I am unfamiliar with post-1900 culture. What is a 'Dalek'?

Traffic cone on the A66. *Get innnn!!!*

New speaking clock markets

Draft excluder.

You know it only works if you lie in front of the door, right?

Oh.

BoJo's Woe Show

Edition **137**

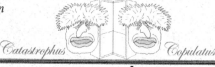

*Crapping on Britain
since August 2019*

Catastrophus — Copulatus

14th Oct 2020

With self-imposed hard Brexit looming ever closer, colossal queues of trucks are (correctly) predicted in Kent and elsewhere.	In an uncharacteristically humanit--arian move, they consider providing stranded drivers with toilets.

BoJo's Woe Show

Edition **138**

Crapping on Britain
since August 2019

15th Oct 2020

Catastrophus *Copulatus*

Colossal amounts of money are given to companies like SERCO to (badly) run track and trace and other pandemic related services.

These companies seldom seem to have any expertise in the area, but do tend to have friends in very high places.

My tooth is in agony!! I need to see a dentist!!

I'll book you an appointment with Mr Serco.

OK shall I sit in the chair?

First, give me a million pounds.

Right! Good. Now come back in six months.

What?? Behh behh but you haven't done anything!!

Haven't I? Gosh! You must have not given me enough money. Another million should do it.

OK That's us done. See you in six months!

Whine! I don't understand it! I paid him 2 million, and I'm still in utter agony! He didn't do *anything*!

Yes he did!

He bought a huge holiday home in the Caribbean and says I can holiday there with him there any time I want. I'd say that's pretty good value for money – especially as none of it was mine.

BoJo's Woe Show

Edition **139**

Crapping on Britain since August 2019

16th Oct 2020

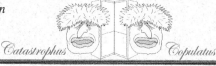

Catastrophus *Copulatus*

Johnson continues his crazy campaign to get either an impossibly favourable trade deal (ruled out by UK red lines) or a No Deal he can blame others for.

The result at this point is to claim a deal that is technically not a deal at all.

BoJo's Woe Show

Edition **140**

*Crapping on Britain
since August 2019*

Catastrophus — *Copulatus*

19th Oct 2020

Brexit ideology looks like a being boon to criminals of all kinds, but don't worry, Gove reckons "alternative methods" will catch them.

Summer exam chaos blamed on "mutant algorithm" (and certainly not the utter morons in charge).

I now understand that what you actually wanted in your leader was a lazy lying f****r who did no actual work …

… other than running get-rich-quick schemes for all of his mates.

Why didn't you tell me? ****I**** *could have been that person, if you'd asked!!*

Did you have a question, you old failure?

Uh, yes. how will we catch criminals, when No Deal will lose us access to EU criminal databases?

No no it'll be much easier! We can use *alternative methods*!

For example, I can walk into my cupboard, put on a police costume, step through the magic door and be a policeman for a day.

Or we could … err…

I know! I know!!!! I made up this *mutant algorithm* to identify the worst criminals in Britain!! It's great! It's made a list already!!

Show me!

You idiot!! That's a list of cabinet members.

No it's not! It's got Dom Cummings and Dido Harding on it too, look!

The point is moot. From 1st January we shall be using an alternative definition of the term "criminal".

As a person who speaks out against Brexit.

BoJo's Woe Show

Edition **141**

*Crapping on Britain
since August 2019*

Catastrophus — *Copulatus*

20th Oct 2020

With his promised "oven ready" deal never anything more than a lie and a fantasy, Johnson tries to force a No Deal Brexit in a way that looks like the EU's fault.

He fails.

Phwaff!!! We've had to end the EU Brexit deal talks because the EU refused to intensify them.

We are willing to intensify the talks.

Well we can't resume the talks anyway, because they won't talk about fishing!

We are willing to talk about fishing.

Oh. Errr … Errr … we … ahhh ah ahhh can't resume the talks … because … we … errr… because I don't like the colour of Barnier's suit!

This'll get 'em! I demand that Barnier dances a perfect cha-cha-cha during every negotiation!!

Francine, could you book me some ballroom dancing lessons, please.

Damn them!!!! Why do they have to keep being so *reasonable*!!!!

BoJo's Woe Show

Edition 142

Crapping on Britain since August 2019

22nd Oct 2020

Catastrophus *Copulatus*

Marcus Rashford, Labour, and other "do-gooders" outrageously suggest that poor children should not be allowed to starve.

Liverpool Mayor asks for money to help people in his city.

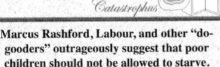

Bloody Burnham!! How *dare* he ask for 60 million pounds!! He hasn't even donated to party funds!!

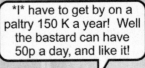

I have to get by on a paltry 150 K a year! Well the bastard can have 50p a day, and like it!

You do know it's for Liverpool, and he's not keeping it for himself?

Not keeping it himself?? Sorry I don't understand.

And now Rashford and Labour want money to feed poor children!!

Well Rashford and Labour can f**k off!!! We can't just magic up cash at will! Let the children starve!!

Ah, Lord Cashface. 263 million, was it? Phwaff!! Here you are. Remind me what it was for?

It's to write a few newspaper articles, explaining why you can't afford to feed children this Xmas.

Ah yes. Essential work!

Ooh! Ooh!! I've had an idea. Raab! Send the RAF to bomb the hell out of a Middle Eastern country!

Uhh, which one?

Don't care. You choose.

What's the plan?

Well, we've got Death, Famine and Pestilence already here. Might as well collect the full set.

Churchill never managed *that*.

BoJo's Woe Show

Edition **143**

Crapping on Britain since August 2019

Catastrophus　　*Copulatus*

28th Oct 2020

If you want to know how bad a state a country is in, look at the things it tries to present as good news.

To find real Brexit benefits, go to European cities outside the UK.

Bozz!! I've found it!! **I've found it!!!** Yippeeee!!

What have you found, Fox?

A real **Brexit benefit!!** At last!! Only took four years!!

Oh my God!! Really???

Soy Sauce!! It's going to be cheaper because of no tariffs with Japan!!

New grasping at straws markets!!

But that's just the same as before!

Oh!

Hang on! '*Just the same*' is really good, right! Because we've completely wrecked everything else!

Shut up you total bloody moron!

Well it's *nearly* a benefit! It's the only thing that isn't going to get *more* expensive!!

Actually a lot of our soy sauce comes from the EU, so it will.

Bugger.

So what your saying is, the closest thing we have to a Brexit benefit is something that isn't really a benefit, and also applies only to people who import all their soy sauce from Japan?

It's the only benefit anyone's ever found.

Unless you're *us*, of course!!

New gravy train markets!!

BoJo's Woe Show

Edition **144**

*Crapping on Britain
since August 2019*

Catastrophus   *Copulatus*

31st Oct 2020

Far too late, the Tories eventually locked down during the second virus wave.

The measure was still widely supported among the public, but there was much more resistance than there had been in the spring.

Everyone hates us!! The Tories all hate the lockdown, and everyone else … just hates us! I don't understand! Everyone was willing to do it in the spring!

What changed??

We probably should try and stop so many people dying. It looks bad. Let's increase the lockdown!

B-but then the tabloids will attack us even *more*!!

Not for long. We'll just randomly open up again in December, and "*save Xmas*"

Great plan! So we lock down now?

Nahh, pick a day next week. I want to do a quick road trip first.

Phwaff!! Next Wednesday, we go up to Tier 4 **straight away**!! I've no idea what that means, but it's a lot stricter than Tier 3!!

Oh hang on, Wednesday's bondage night at *Madame Spanky's*

We'll be going straight up to Tier 4 on **Thursday morning**!!

BoJo's Woe Show

Edition **145**

*Crapping on Britain
since August 2019*

Catastrophus   *Copulatus*

8th Nov 2020

After a tortuous wait while postal votes are counted (Trump tried to obstruct this), Biden wins US election by 7 million votes. | Johnson's message of congratulation fails to impress because a last minute correction is still visible.

What are you lot grizzling about??

It's Donald!!   Boo Hoo!

He's lost!!   Sob!!

No no, don't be silly, he *won*!! He called me to say so! He won bigly!!

Now I know this is hard for you to grasp, but Donald was lying to you, because he's not really your friend. Only *I* am really your friend.

Trump's a moron. He'd have won if he'd let Dido Harding oversee the counting of postal votes, like I suggested.

Now I'm afraid you're going to really hate the next bit.

(which is a silver lining, I guess …)

I can't do it, I can't do it, **I can't do it**!! Sob!!

Well you have to!!

For goodness' sake, you pathetic fat lump! You've said thousands of things you don't mean in your life! What's so hard about **this one?**

Don't know, sir.

I even typed the bloody message for you! All you have to do is hit 'send'!

Go on, you can do it!! Imagine you're booking a dirty weekend, or something.

Gnnnnhhhh …

Congratulations on winning the election, ~~Donald~~. Please let us have a nice US trade deal? Pleeeeeeease!!!

Your loyal friend, Boris

Crapping on Britain since August 2019

12th Nov 2020

Catastrophus *Copulatus*

Dom appoints his best mate Lee Cain to the Downing Street staff, even though the other boss, Carrie, hates him.

A tug-of-hate ensues, which will soon lead to a change of leadership for the UK …

This is Lee Cain. I've decided he's going to be your new Downing Street chief of staff, because frankly I'm sick of the sight of you, so he'll be helping to babysit you, now.

But … ahhh…. This is a bit of a sticky one … thing is … Carrie doesn't like him.

WHAT? Who's in charge, here, you useless ball of snot?

Y-you of course. (and her)

L-l-look… she says that he's a **Vote Leave** guy. His only talent is getting weak and gullible people to do stupid things that'll make their lives worse!

Oh well, no hard feelings. Hey, why don't you sneak off for a lockdown-breaking dirty weekend with some Russian prostitutes, film the whole thing, and give Dom the tape?

Great idea!!

See? Still got it!

I'll have your contract drawn up.

DAYS LATER…

Fired? What do you mean, he's been **fired**?! I gave no such order!!

Hey fatty!! You fired Cain! You're in *so much trouble now!*

Whine!! It was Carrie! She made me do it!!

What do you mean, you re-hired him? Why can't you ever *stand up for yourself*???

D-don't know, miss.

BoJo's Woe Show

Edition **147**

*Crapping on Britain
since August 2019*

13th Nov 2020

Catastrophus   *Copulatus*

Cummings dramatically exits No 10, carrying a box that looks like it might contain a severed head (it doesn't).

For the next year he will snipe from the sidelines, attacking both progressive causes and Johnson's epic incompetence.

BoJo's Woe Show

Edition **148**

Crapping on Britain since August 2019

Catastrophus   Copulatus

14th Nov 2020

With Dominic Cummings gone, will Johnson finally take charge of his own destiny?

Johnson is said by those who know him to hold no political opinions beyond those of the last person he spoke to, whoever that was.

Freeeee!!!! I'm *free*!! Free at last to make my own choices and be my **own man**!

To set my own agenda!!

So I'm going to use my premiership to … errr … do things like … ummm….

Save fluffy animals, and actually spend time with your current family.

YES! I shall now be the kitten-saving, **family man PM**!

No, no, what you *really* want to do is strangle kittens, dismember puppies, starve the poor, and deport people.

Yes!!! I shall be kitten and puppy slaughtering, food-snatching, UKIP PM, and people will love me for it!

Actually Boris, what you've really wanted to be all your life is a socialist!

Yes!!! *This* is who I am! Tax the rich! Help the poor! *We'll keep the red flag flyyyyying!!*

I have a better idea…

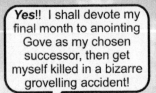

Yes!! I shall devote my final month to anointing Gove as my chosen successor, then get myself killed in a bizarre grovelling accident!

Note for you, PM.

Oh **YES**!! What a great idea!!

People of Britain!! I have decided that I shall devote my premiership to flushing my own head down the toilet, and giving billion pound contracts to Dominic Cummings, that don't require him to do anything.

BoJo's Woe Show

Edition **149**

*Crapping on Britain
since August 2019*

15th Nov 2020

Catastrophus  *Copulatus*

Who will replace Cummings? | **Do YOU have what it takes to enter …** *The C Factor?*

Boris you lazy toad! Get back to work **right now,** or I'll spank your arse till it bleeds!!!

I am not convinced.

It's a no from me.

A bit too emotional.

NEXT!!

THE C FACTOR

Now Boris, you need to … err … oh … I've forgotten.

NEXT!!

Johnson, you're a stupid, nasty, evil, traitorous, smelly, egotistical, self-serving, no-good heap of dog turds!!! You're a **disgrace**, and anyone who voted for you is a **total moron**!!!

We can't possibly make *you* Boris's new handler, Jeremy!

I know. I just really wanted the chance to say it!

Fair enough. NEXT!!

Boris, Boris, wherefor art thou Boris? … I'm really *not* a racist, you know!

NEXT!!

H …

NEXT!!

Sob!! Give me a chance!!

Right! Do as I say, boss, or I'll get my great big tarantula out of my pocket and … oh … hang on …

It's in my pants!! It's *in my pants!!* Aaaarrrggghhh! Get it out, GET IT OUT!!!

NEXT!!

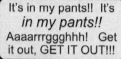

Just shut up and do as you're told, you useless fat blob of elephant snot!!

Perfect!

When can you start, Mr …?

Dommings. Cuminic Dommings.

BoJo's Woe Show

Edition **150**

*Crapping on Britain
since August 2019*

Catastrophus   Copulatus

19th Nov 2020

Signs of Carrie's very light green influence start to appear in some of Johnson's random policy suggestions.

The rest of the time, its Brexitty shaft-the-country business as usual.

Phwaff!! I'm pleased to announce a spend of 3 billion pounds to very slightly cut our carbon emissions!

UNDER NEW MANAGEMENT

And also 16 billion pounds on building things to **blow people up!!**

Ahh ahh and 30 billion for a few posh people to build a giant nursing home for elderly hedgehogs and other cute and cuddly animals!

UNDER NEW

And 50 billion on **more bombs** *while everyone starves!! Bhwah hah hahh!*

UNDER NEW MANAGEMENT

80 billion on **kitten sanctuaries!**

UNDER NEW MANAGEMENT

120 billion on impossible to understand settlement forms for EU nationals!

UNDER NEW

Get lost, Cummings!! You're not in charge here anymore! I am! I won!!

Sorry to disappoint you, princess nut-nuts!! You may have kicked me out of Downing Street, but you'll never kick me out of here!!

Oh yeah?   *Yeah!!*

UNDER NEW MANAGEMENT

Ehh bweh bwehhh bwehhh ... phwaff!! Wibble!! Wehh wehh Winston Churchill! ... Scottish people smell ... er ... er ...

Where's all this money going to come from, Prime Minister!?

BIFF! BASH! THUMP!

UNDER NEW

BoJo's Woe Show

Edition **151**

Crapping on Britain
since August 2019

Catastrophus   *Copulatus*

20th Nov 2020

Report reveals that Priti Patel has been bullying members of the civil service, another breach of ministerial code.

Johnson predictably ignores all these misdeeds and so the report's author, seeing his role as pointless, feels forced to resign.

Now Patel, about these bullying allegations …

Biffabaconnus servus-civilis.

Who's been squealin' now? I'll crush his balls in a nutcracker!!!

It's all lies!!! I **never** forced them to surrender their dinner money!! They gave it up willingly!! And when we gave Sir Hilary a wedgie, it was just larkin' around!!

You have been bullying the entire Civil Service, Patel.

Vindictus maximus est.

Oh yeah, Mr Speccy Teacher's Pet? You gonna stop me, huh?

How are you goin' to do that when I've stamped on your glasses and flushed your head down the toilet?

Don't think I haven't seen you sneakin' off to the bogs with those prints of Victorian sweat shops!!

If you'd listen … you've done nothing wrong. Nonetheless, we feel that a change of jobs for you is desirable.

Bite me, you ****in' pretentious twat!!

It is NOT a demotion. It is simply that a vacancy has arisen, to which you are uniquely suited…

Johnson, you pathetic lump of maggot droppings!!! Stop faffing around, and get on with those **cuts**!! The poor won't starve themselves, you feeble worm!! Do I have to get out my **garlic crusher** again?

Wh- whimper!!

Bah! Turns out I'm **not** irreplaceable.

BoJo's Woe Show

Edition 152

Crapping on Britain since August 2019

Catastrophus — *Copulatus*

25th Nov 2020

| Tories break manifesto pledge by cutting foreign aid. | Bizarre video emerges of Johnson celebrating. | Sheep farmers protest that Brexit barriers will destroy them. |

I'm pleased to announce that we are cutting foreign aid, and breaking yet another manifesto promise!

Ohhh yeah, baby!!!

It'll probably lead to countless preventable deaths, but we don't care, really. We have to look after our own.

So does this mean you'll use the money to let the poorest kids in Britain eat this Xmas, after all?

What?? Of course not!!!

We'll be giving it all to some more of our super-rich mates, in return for a few holiday homes and some big party donations.

Looking after our own, you know?

£££

PM! Brexit is going to bankrupt our sheep farmers! The backbenchers are unhappy. They want you to do something to help!

Backbenchers worrying about sheep? Phwaff! Well why don't we just replace them all with cows!

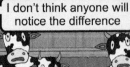

I don't think anyone will notice the difference

Cows?

Yes.

Mooooooo!!!!

BoJo's Woe Show

*Crapping on Britain
since August 2019*

Catastrophus   *Copulatus*

26th Nov 2020

Tory cronyism reaches full-on absurdity as Matt Hancock gives major Covid contract to his pub landlord.	If I'd made that up, I might have been told it was too far fetched. But he actually did. And of course wasn't fired for it.

Guys! Guys!! I've solved the pandemic!!

This bloke I met down the pub is cooking up a whole batch of virus tests for us in his cellar! Only cost half a billion, cash in hand.

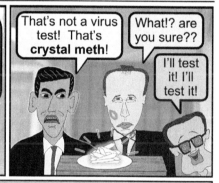

That's not a virus test! That's **crystal meth**!

What!? are you sure??

I'll test it! I'll test it!

So now we've got half a billion pounds' worth of *crystal meth*?

Let's send it all to China as **foreign aid**. We used to do that with opium, in the **good old days**!

I know! I know!! Let's sell it all in schools! I don't know much about schools, but I've seen it on the telly!! You can make loads of money selling this stuff to kids!!

Tell you what, Williamson, why don't you give that a go yourself?

SHORTLY...

Don't worry, Gavin. We'll bail you out just as soon as we've paid off the national debt.

Now, how are those 16 billion's worth of warships and bombs coming on?

It's sorted! Guy next door said he'd do it, so I gave him the cash.

Next door to *you*? But isn't that? ...

AND IN THE CAYMAN ISLANDS

Send Mr Sunak a few matchstick models of warships ... And tell him I'll be back for a few days next year, if I can be bothered.

Yes boss.

BoJo's Woe Show

Edition **154**

*Crapping on Britain
since August 2019*

30th Nov 2020

Catastrophus  *Copulatus*

With farmers all over Britain facing ruin because of Brexit, Johnson (and her fat husband) try to spin this as a plus, giving land back to nature.

It's just a shame that food imports are being hit by Brexit at the same time. Empty shelves, here we come!

Thanks to Brexit, we'll be turning all our farms back to nature! Phwaff!

Keep going!

Ahh ahh and there'll be new woods! full of cuddly frolicking rabbits and squirrels and hedgehogs!! Phwaff!! Lovely!!

Ohhh, I love it when you pretend to be green!

Ooooh, yeah!

B-but PM, what'll we eat?

Waitrose organic, of course! We'll be keeping *those* farms.

And everyone else?

What? Why would I care about *them*?

Well if the people all start starving to death, it might cost us a few votes in the marginals

Fickle bastards!! How ungrateful can you get?

We've got those dried yak intestines coming in from Mongolia – isn't that enough?

Nowhere near.

Maybe the problem's not too little food, but too many people?

Good point! Call the papers, tell them we're relaxing the virus rules completely over Xmas!

BoJo's Woe Show

Edition **155**

Crapping on Britain since August 2019

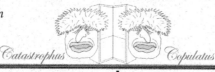

Catastrophus — Copulatus

2nd Dec 2020

Johnson is seen looking haggard on the Parliamentary benches, like a tramp who wandered in out of the cold.

It is an image that reflects reality far more than the clown persona that so many are taken in by.

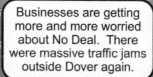

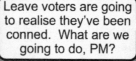

… and for those brief moments, the Prime Minister saw himself for who and what he truly was.

BoJo's Woe Show

Edition **156**

Crapping on Britain since August 2019

3rd Dec 2020

Catastrophus · *Copulatus*

Education secretary Gavin "Frank Spencer" Williamson tries to claim that Britain is the best country in the world.

A year later, the Tories will revise this message to "we're not corrupt, honest" and "other countries are more corrupt than us" …

Britain is the **best country!!** The best country in the **world!**

YES!!! What other country would be able to deport a whole planeload of people to Jamaica, even though none of the poor bastards have ever lived there!! *Go Britain! Go me!!*

Err…. where was I? Oh Yes! Britain! We're such nice people! Great people! *World-beating!*

Phwaff!! That's right, only this week we signed a lovely trade deal with **North Macedonia!**

New olive oil markets!!!

For them.

There, you see? That'll pay off the national debt in no time. Britain!! We're brilliant!! We're even keeping exams next year, *how good is that?!*

Except in Wales.

Wales? Is that part of Britain, now?

We've *definitely* got the best education system in the world!

Where else could a guy like *me* become a senior government minister? Huh? *Tell me that!*

I heard it happened in Burundi, once.

Fictional countries don't count.

BoJo's Woe Show

Edition **157**

*Crapping on Britain
since August 2019*

3rd Dec 2020

Catastrophus — *Copulatus*

Perhaps the most shameless Tory lie of all time: the claim that Brexit enabled the early vaccine success. In fact it was the NHS.

Sadly, many in the media failed to challenge the lie, including some BBC presenters.

BoJo's Woe Show

Edition **158**

Crapping on Britain
since August 2019

Catastrophus   *Copulatus*

4ᵗʰ Dec 2020

| Shapps decides to exempt rich businessmen from quarantine rules. | After all, they're exempt from most other rules in Tory Britain. | Time for a grilling from Kay Burley. |

Grant Shapps, you're exempting "high value" business travellers from quarantine rules. So do you regard everyone else as being "low value"?

Well, *duhhh*! Of course we do. We're the Tories.

But business travellers come in and out far more than everyone else. So you're enabling super-spreader events, aren't you?

Can we talk about the A66 instead?

No.

OK, well, we can solve that problem by vaccinating all the "high value" people first, instead of nurses and all the other "low value" people.

So you're using Covid to introduce a policy of health inequality to Britain, aren't you?

Goodness me, no! Where have you been for the last ten years? Health inequality has *always* been our policy whenever we've been in power!

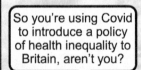

But when it comes to Covid, you're saying that only the poor have to self - isolate?

Well that's just not true, Kay, because thanks to Brexit …

The whole country is going to be self-isolating from 1ˢᵗ January!!

BoJo's Woe Show

Edition **159**

Crapping on Britain since August 2019

4th Dec 2020

Catastrophus *Copulatus*

Liz *"New Pork Markets"* Truss is voted most popular Tory in a poll of party members.

Inexplicably, Dominic Raab comes 4th, but even Tory members can only tolerate so much incompetence …

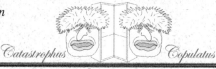

Yesssss!!! I'm the **best**!! They like me **best**!

You're holdin' it upside down, Williamson, you pathetic little snivellin' turd. You came **last**.

Whaaat?

But *I* didn't win, either. How many plebs do I have to deport, to win this thing?

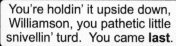

Phwaff! Don't take it too hard, Cruella. Not everyone can be as universally loved as *me*!

You came 4th from last.

WHAT? How dare they?! So who won?

New big-headedness Markets!!!

Ungrateful s**ts!!! I cut off trade from *all of Europe*, and what thanks do I get? She partially restores it with North Macedonia, and the bastards love her! *It's so unfair!!*

New sour grapes markets!

Cheer up, fatty! At least you narrowly beat the guy who oversaw 60 000 deaths as Health Secretary!

Well I'm glad Sunak didn't win. Where did he come?

Second. He's not taking it very well.

Boo hoo hoooo!

BoJo's Woe Show

Edition **160**

Crapping on Britain since August 2019

Catastrophus   *Copulatus*

9th Dec 2020

Michael Gove has told a series of provable lies since 2016.

Gove is one of the very few competent members of Johnson's Cabinet of Horrors and so possibly the most dangerous.

Michael Gove, you promised that Brits would be able to freely live and work in the EU after Brexit. That was a lie, wasn't it?

Well, it's a complex issue, but the people have spoken.

So that's a yes, then.

Boris vowed that there'd be no border on the Irish Sea. But now you've agreed to one.

Um, will of the people.

Your party even lied to the Queen!

She's a bloody Remainer. She deserved it.

You promised, repeatedly, that environmental and animal welfare standards would be retained post Brexit, then ditched them at the first sniff of a trade deal.

Ah, but Rees Mogg said we'd bin the lot, and we're keeping **his** promise.

And you promised to resign if the internal Market Bill was watered down. So why are you still in your job?

Listen, you fool, we're the Tories! People don't expect us to tell the truth, or keep our promises!

When you voted us in, you voted to be lied to. You voted to have your rights taken away. You voted to be treated like dirt, and now we will oblige!

So remember, all the awful things that are about to happen are **YOUR** fault, whether you voted for us or not.

BoJo's Woe Show

Edition **161**

*Crapping on Britain
since August 2019*

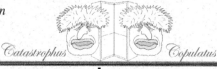

Catastrophus   *Copulatus*

11th Dec 2020

Commentators increasingly (and correctly) predict empty shelves due to Brexit.

The Tories all shrug it off. It may be their fault, but they know it won't harm any of them personally.

No, I'm not the slightest bit worried about food shortages and empty shelves after a No Deal Brexit.

I mean, whatever happens, *I'll* be alright.

Anyone facing a deficiency of sustenance can go and slaughter some game on one of their private estates.

Or have a servant do it.

Or simply have a pizza delivered to them from Italy, by private jet.

And if they're *not* millionaires?

Sorry, I don't understand the question.

Look, the plebs won't starve. There'll be lots of mutton from all the sheep farms that go bust. Then beef and pork a bit later.

And after that … uhhhh…

Let them eat cats!

New cannibalism markets!

Or make homebrew out of socksh!

As we speak, Boris is working *flat out*, two hours a week, to deal with this crisis, by tricking voters into blaming anyone but us.

Don't worry everyone! We're getting an **Australian style** deal, remember? And it comes with **Australian style** food …

Why-aye, man! In today's **Brexit-tucker trial**, starving Brits will be eating fried ants, cockroaches, and rats' testicles!

BoJo's Woe Show

Edition **162**

Crapping on Britain since August 2019

13th Dec 2020

Catastrophus Copulatus

Johnson seems to swing between desperation for a deal and plotting for No Deal.

During one of the former phases, Johnson flies to Brussels to plead his case with Ursula von der Leyen.

Phwaff!!! I'll have **four navy warships**, to ahh ahhh ahhhhh **defend my fish!!** Yes!!

The options are chips or sauteed potatoes, Monsieur.

Oh. In that case, I'll have ah ahh ahhhh **magic beans**, that will grow a bean-stalk where at the top I'll find the ***exact same benefits*** as full EU membership!

Mr Johnson, I do not feel that you are taking this meeting entirely seriously.

I am!! I really am It's just .... ahhh ... a little bit stuck here. Made a lot of promises, you see ... full sovereignty ... frictionless trade ...

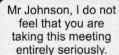

help me.

Sigh.

You "*lied to please the mob*", Mr Johnson, and now you must either tell them the truth, or let them find it out for themselves.

I know!!! We'll tell them I died! Choked on a French fishbone! Yes!! I'll hide out on St Helena for 50 years until the first Brexit benefit appears!!

BoJo's Woe Show

Edition **163**

*Crapping on Britain
since August 2019*

Catastrophus   *Copulatus*

16th Dec 2020

Johnson responds to reasonable questions by attacking peoples' right to question him at all.

He deflects any criticism of him by calling it an attack on British institutions (but claims any credit for himself, of course).

Bwehhhh bwehhh bwehhh … phwaff!!! You're totally trivializing the efforts of the British people … heroic nurses … blitz spirit!! Instead of asking nasty questions you should be supporting the government! So there!

Perhaps you didn't hear the question, so I'll ask it again …

Have you changed Wilbur's nappy, or haven't you?

Well, thehhh thehhhh thehhhhh this has been an **unprecedentedly challenging** year for nappy changing, being actually in the same house as one of my babies six months later, couldn't have predicted that, and …

Answer the bloody question!!!!

Oh … I've … ahh … just had a call from Liz Truss! Off to, ahh, negotiate a trade deal with India. *New elephant markets*, yes! Back in March. Sure you can all manage without me until then!

Come back you feckless bastard!!!

Don't worry. I'll take on **all** of Boris' duties while he's away. Though I'll delegate the nappies of course.

I'll help! I'll help!!

I put the baby in the dishwasher and the nappy in the fridge. That's right, isn't it?

BoJo's Woe Show

Edition **164**

*Crapping on Britain
since August 2019*

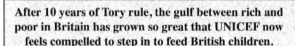

17th Dec 2020

Catastrophus   *Copulatus*

After 10 years of Tory rule, the gulf between rich and poor in Britain has grown so great that UNICEF now feels compelled to step in to feed British children.

Rees Mogg objects – not to the poverty of course, but to people trying to help.

It is a total disgrace for UNICEF to be feeding British children. It is playing politics, a political stunt of the lowest order.

Little children should be **seen and not heard**, and hungry children, doubly so.

Those interfering UNICEF do-gooders need to understand that the British people elected a **Tory government**, which means they voted for poor people to starve, and we **will** deliver on that commitment.

*Starvatum infantium
optandum est.*

If UNICEF truly wish to assist the needy in these difficult times, I can point them towards a number of hedge fund managers, who stand to lose large sums if Boris unwisely agrees a deal with the EU.

Not to mention a rather large number of posh children whose father is too impoverished to properly support them!

I told you, **get lost**! If you try to prove it's my kid, I'll send **every single tabloid** to your front door! You want that? Do you??

BoJo's Woe Show

Edition **165**

Crapping on Britain since August 2019

17th Dec 2020

Catastrophus Copulatus

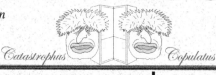

Britain has become a plague island as the virus gets out of control. Other countries respond by closing the borders with the UK.

Flights are cancelled, and ports grind to a standstill.

All the other countries are closing their borders with us! There's chaos at the ports!

Well there was already!

Oh. Yes. But now it's even worse!

The country is going to run out of food!!

Well we could all drink plebs' blood, instead.

I know! I know! Let's all just go to a school and push in at the dinner queue!

If there's no food, there won't **be** any school dinners, you total moron. Which would save us some money, I suppose.

But not enough! The economy is going into freefall!

Brilliant!!!

It's the perfect cover for **No Deal**!! The plebs won't even notice the difference! I don't know why we didn't think of this earlier!

A highly agreeable outcome. Soon all but the very rich will be going hungry! It is most uplifting! *Miseria plebii pro mihi elatio est!*

But we shall need the RAF in the air …

… to stop the cursed UNICEF from dropping any food parcels to spoil my happiness!

Johnson you incompetent bastard!!

All my deportation flights have been cancelled! You've **completely** ruined my Xmas!!!

BoJo's Woe Show

Edition **166**

Crapping on Britain since August 2019

Catastrophus *Copulatus*

21st Dec 2020

Respected journalist Pippa Crerar asks Johnson straightforward questions during a press briefing. | **He responds with gobbledegook about "parallel universes." Apparently Tory voters are fine with this.**

Ehh bweh bwehhhh … phwaff!! Lot of virus about … ehhh veh vehhh … all be over by Easter! German car makers to the rescue! Rehh Rule Brittania, and all that.

So why has Dover descended into abject chaos?

Nehhh nehhh no, no, not descended. Phwaff!! **Ascended**! Yes!! Dover has **ascended**, because all this chaos was … ahhhh … carefully planned!! I think that's what I mean, anyway.

But why do you keep over-promising and under-delivering?

Well I don't as much under-deliver as … over … ahhh … under … over … underground … overground … Wombling free … or rather, over … under ... Uber! That's it! We're going to *Uber-deliver*! Phwaff! Get someone else to deliver and they get hardly any money while I trouser the rest for not actually doing anything, which is ahh ahh absolutely a stable form of government in this country.

BORIS   ARSE   ELBOW

Yehh you have to … ahhhh… imagine in a parallel universe, where … where … Rees Mogg has a soul, Patel has a Heart, and Williamson has a brain, and wehhh we're all going to see the Wizard of Oz, and he's going to give us a Brexit deal with all the same benefits as we had in 2016, aaand…

… yes, I think that, yes I've answered your question completely there.

Thehh theh thank you and good night.

BoJo's Woe Show

Edition **167**

Crapping on Britain since August 2019

22nd Dec 2020

Catastrophus   Copulatus

| Johnson won the election mainly by lying, and has told numerous provable lies during his time as PM. | Keen to avoid all consequences from his constant lying, he seeks to pollute the Lords with people who are as dishonest as he is. |

BoJo's Woe Show

Edition **168**

*Crapping on Britain
since August 2019*

Xmas 2020

Catastrophus *Copulatus*

Johnson is a man who'll promise everything and deliver nothing.	**The "oven-ready" Brexit deal was merely one example of this.**	**Some people worked this out a lot faster than others.**

BoJo's Woe Show

Edition **169**

*Crapping on Britain
since August 2019*

Catastrophus · Copulatus

Xmas 2020

Tories enjoy Xmas, with food, presents and family.	Meanwhile hundreds of EU truck drivers spend festive period stuck in massive jams caused by Tory policy.	A year later, Tories will wonder why so few want to work in the UK.

BoJo's Woe Show

Edition **170**

*Crapping on Britain
since August 2019*

End of Dec 2020

Catastrophus   *Copulatus*

Johnson has secured a woeful Brexit deal, basically May's deal but with extra concessions to EU. | Most Tory MPs vote it through without reading it (well it was Xmas) but will everyone accept it? | The ERG is a far right grouping within the Tories.

Phwaff!! I know this Brexit deal wasn't everything you hoped for. I admit it isn't *quite* what I promised …

It reduces GDP by 5%, and makes almost everyone poorer. Except tax-dodging billionaires, of course.

Leh lehhh lehhh lots of businesses are going bust or moving abroad, and hundreds of billions of pounds of government money is flowing into the pockets of vulture capitalists.

We've destabilized Northern Ireland and set back international co-operation by decades, making it far harder to catch white collar criminals!

Ahhh ahh and we've stripped young people of the chance to work, live, and study abroad.

So I really have done a *lot* of what you asked for!! I-I-I-know you wanted it to go even further, but *please*, ERG! Please back my little deal?

Give us your first born child to devour, and we will consider it.

I d-don't know which one that is.

Coming soon …

BoJo's Woe Show

Editions **171** onwards

Drowning Britain in untreated sewage since August 2019   Books **4** and **5**: Jan-Dec 2021

THE WOE GOES ON …

At the time of writing, Boris Johnson is somehow still Prime Minister, thanks in no small part to members of the public who bleat that he is "doing his best" in response to any kind of criticism. (That's a pretty low bar, if you think about it). However, following the Owen Paterson scandal, some voters may finally have woken up to his unparalleled awfulness. Will he make it much further? We shall see.

This means there will be at least two more *Woe Show* books to enjoy! From their dystopian plans to stamp all over protest and democracy, through the malignant chaos of GB News, to Kermit the Frog, Peppa Pig and the comical end of Hancock's tenure, there are many more stories to tell of Britain's most ridiculous ever political leader (and her useless fat husband).

ABOUT THE AUTHOR:
Dr Richard Milne is an evolutionary plant biologist whose eclectic CV includes ~80 scientific papers, the novel '*Misjudgement Day*' (see following pages), a factual book called '*Rhododendron*' (Reaktion Books), scripting 6 cartoon strips for Viz, and three awards from students for his off-beat teaching style. You can experience this yourself by searching for "*Can nettles swim? The riddle of how plants cross oceans*" on Youtube.

He has drawn over 500 cartoons on Twitter, but if you bought this book, you probably know that. He apologises unreservedly for the long gap between books, that is largely because as well as his full time job as a science lecturer, he is also a devoted dad and is working on a free ID tool for the British flora, which involves photographing every plant species found wild in Britain (Google "Weebly Milneorchid" for what exists so far). Busy times!

Stay tuned to @milneorchid on Twitter for all the latest updates!
Now turn the page for some bonus material …

"Suzy McCabe's going to let you do THAT?"

"Yep."

"All weekend?"

"That's what she said," said Michael. He was sitting with Roger in a quiet corner of the bar in the Stoke University Student Union Bar. Michael had short neat hair and a smart shirt, whereas Roger as always sported precisely messed up hair, and a t-shirt advertising a band only he had heard of.

"This is Suzy 'Piss off, you're not rich enough' McCabe we're talking about?" asked Roger.

"She'd booked a dirty weekend away with some posh git, but he's got mumps."

"Mumps?"

"Mumps. Making a comeback, apparently. So she needed a stand-in, and I, Michael Price, am rising to the occasion."

"I can see that," said Roger, leaning back on his chair. "It's very romantic."

"Bollocks to that! I haven't had a shag since Fresher's week."

"Hence your desperation to get out of this weekend trip."

"I'll owe you big time if I do. Have you got anywhere?"

"I managed to get two people to drop out by offering a full refund, and exaggerating the weather forecast."

"Not that it needed much exaggeration," said Michael. "It looks horrendous."

"So that leaves five committee and two other blokes who certainly want to go. With seven I can make a case for cancellation. But if even one more signs up, there'll be no chance of persuading them. Are you sure you can't just make an excuse and drop out, again?"

Michael sighed and shook his head. "I'm president. Plus there's no other driver for the minibus. If I drop out for the second time in a row, Helen will no-confidence me, and she'll probably win! I still don't know how I won the election in the first place."

"Does it matter?" asked Roger. "I mean, I'd much rather you than her, but do you really need it?"

"CV, Roger. Plus I got two dates out of saying I'm the Pres, even if it is president of the Wacky Walkers club. I'm not dropping out. If we can't get the trip cancelled, I'm using Project Strawberry."

"Oh God, Michael, not that again."

"It'll work, and no-one will accuse me of shirking my responsibilities!"

"Let's just hope we can get it cancelled, okay?"

"I declare this committee meeting of the Stoke University Wacky Walkers open."

"Hang on, Mycroft, the President isn't here yet," said Dylan, the transport secretary, playing with his forelocks. "Nor's the Treasurer, or the Social Secretary."

"That is irrelevant," said Mycroft, club secretary. He wore an immaculate tweed waistcoat over a checked yellow shirt, and sat with his back ramrod straight. "The scheduled start time has come and gone, a point in time specifically selected to permit ample opportunity for all persons to arrive from their preceding activities. The president knows this, and in his absence the vice president is empowered to act in his stead."

"Again," added Dylan, quietly.

"Okay, let's just get on with it," said Helen Black, the vice president, a small girl with short dark hair. She and the two boys were seated in a small dark room in the basement of the Student Union building, surrounded by piles of folding tables. Three more chairs stood empty. "So we need to talk about the weekend – "

"The first item on the agenda is the last meeting's minutes," said Mycroft.

"Approved," chorused Helen and Dylan wearily.

"…and matters arising."

Helen sighed, and was halfway through asking Mycroft to list these matters, when the door swung open and Michael and Roger walked in. "What have you two been conspiring about?" asked Helen.

"Helen, will you leave off with the conspiracy thing?" Michael took his seat.

"I will, when you tell me where all the postal votes in the election came from," replied Helen icily.

"From people who thought I'd do the best job, madam VICE president."

"Fifteen people. None of whom, by your own admission, you have actually met."

"Yes, so they clearly voted based on objective opinions," said Michael, his face set in what he thought was a Prime Ministerial expression.

"They haven't been to a single event between them! Mycroft checked!"

Now Michael looked angry. "Mycroft? Why?"

"The vice president persuaded me that the possibility of foul play was sufficient to warrant further investigation."

"Now see here," said Michael, struggling to keep from shouting. "I had no contact with any of those people. I didn't ask any of them to vote for me, I didn't tell anyone else to …"

"You're missing the point," Helen cut in sharply. "I'm not accusing *you*. I'm saying, what if someone outside the club had decided to interfere?"

If she'd thought this would placate him, she was wrong. "So now you're saying … what? That the Orienteering Club are out to destroy us, by hacking our elections? Or maybe you think it was Vladimir Putin? And that somehow, I'm their unwitting agent of destruction?"

"I'm just saying that it's odd, that fifteen people with no connection to the club, no stake in it, all suddenly decided to vote in this election. Mycroft, how many postal votes were there in the last ten AGMs?"

"Last year, none. The year before, none …"

"In total!"

"Three, over the ten years. Two of which were Richard Hames, who was a regular member, but often had rehearsals on Thursday nights."

"Then suddenly, fifteen," said Helen, her arms folded.

Michael folded his arms as well. "Mycroft, do you have any actual evidence for any of this, anything that would invalidate the election result."

"No," replied Mycroft.

"Then I suggest that we let the matter rest." Michael's eyes challenged Helen to respond, but she did not. "Mycroft, strike everything from the minutes until this point," said Michael.

"Done," said Mycroft. "The first item on the agenda is to approve the last meeting's minutes."

*****

Five minutes later, they finally got to the subject of the weekend trip. "How many do we have signed up, Mycroft?"

"All committee members except Roger," said Mycroft, "plus two others."

"Is that all?" said Helen, in shock. "I thought there were more."

"We had some drop-outs," said Roger.

"Michael, you said you had a plan to recruit people."

"I did. It seems it didn't work."

Mycroft said, "As I stated in my report, which I assume you all read before the meeting, I did as instructed, and composed a precisely worded statement informing the membership that unless at least one further member joined the Arrochar trip, it would be financially unviable and that cancellation would therefore become inevitable," said Mycroft. "It was sent at eight o five GMT yesterday."

"I can't think why no-one responded," said Dylan, nibbling at his fingers.

Mycroft

Helen was looking at Michael curiously. He didn't meet her eye. "Perhaps if we'd knocked on a few doors," she said. "Can we really not absorb the loss?"

Roger the treasurer spoke for the first time. "It would jeopardise all of our remaining events this year. But if we cancel today we can recover all but the deposits."

"And the weather's looking terrible, both days of the weekend," said Michael. "Therefore, I move that –"

The door to the room flew open. "Bernie to the rescue!!!" The improbably named Bernard Wilkinson, club social secretary, danced into the room, spinning twice on his heels as he made for the empty seat beside Dylan. Today he was clad in bright red trousers and a lurid green shirt to match the current shade of his hair. "How's it hanging, cats? Feeling a bit of a negative vibe here, oooh, I am *so* gonna fix that! Bernie saves the day!! Cinderella *shall* go to the ball!"

Michael could feel the disappointment brewing in the area most affected, inside his underpants. "What are you blathering on about, Bernie?"

"Cashflow, darlings. Turning loss into profit! Bums on seats!"

"You mean you've found extra people to come on the trip?" asked Helen.

Bernie pushed his finger into the corner of his mouth, pretending to think. "In a way, Darls, in a way. I've got the most spec-TAC-ular plan, you'll want to have its babies! The Megadance Festival is in Glasgow this weekend." He looked at all the blank faces in the room, shrugged, and went on. "Oh come on! The Megadance! All the Dance Socs who are anybody just *have* to be there. Only our little FolkSoc foursome have a bit of a getting-there problem. Can't afford the train, but then, who can? So I get to thinking, why don't we drive them up and drop them off? Aren't I brilliant?"

"And they'll be paying for the transport?" asked Helen.

"Well it was either that or sexual favours, Darl, but you girls can be *so* touchy about that." He made ready to duck, but Helen was too busy watching Michael to respond. "So yes, good hard cash, duckies," concluded Bernie.

Dylan said: "twenty pounds for each of them would make up for the two who dropped out."

"They're saying sixty between them," said Bernie, "and not a penny more!"

"I can't agree to this without meeting them," said Michael. "And we have to tell the minibus hire people one way or another tonight!"

"Calm yourself, Mikester. Old Bernie's got it in hand." He threw open the door. "Bring on the Dancing Girls!!"

Through the door strode four young ladies. The atmosphere in the room changed completely as it filled with things never normally associated with Wacky Walkers events: make-up, heeled shoes, perfume, jewellery, and skirts. Michael said nothing, hoping the mutual awkwardness would scupper the deal.

"Oh, where are my manners?" said Bernie. "Ooh, if Mumsie could see me now there'd be stern words, I tell you. Stern words. Michael, Helen, Mycroft, Roger and Dylan … I present to you Lucy, Janelle, Lysandra and Natalia."

"So, you're the Pres, huh?" grunted Lucy to Michael, in a gritty voice utterly at odds with her colourful, feminine outfit. She had a round face and brown curly hair.

"Uh, yes," he replied, feeling that events were out of his control.

"Sixty pounds, there and back. To the door, mind. I'm not having my girls getting soaked trying to find the bloody place. And you pick us up four thirty Sunday. Pronto."

"Now hold on a minute," said Michael.

Mycroft spoke up. "Owing to the vagaries of hillwalking, including such possibilities as minor injuries reducing the speed of a group, which must progress at the rate of its slowest member, we cannot guarantee to you a precise pick-up time. Furthermore traffic problems introduce an additional confounding variable. Therefore you would be advised to find some hostelry in which to await our arrival, which we shall endeavour to expedite as close as possible to your allotted time."

Lucy shrugged and nodded. Bernie rubbed his hands with glee. Helen declared, "I say we do it," and Dylan readily agreed.

Defeated, Michael accepted the plan and shook Lucy's hand. Then a thought struck him. "Do any of you girls drive minibuses?"

The front three girls shook their heads, but the one at the back, Natalia, raised a hand. "I nearly drive one time for Russian Society. They say is okay because I have license and drive big tractor in home. Then trip is cancel."

Michael asked, "but you've driven in this country before?"

"I drive in Mother Russia many time."

"Good, well, it's always nice to have a spare driver in case one of us breaks a leg or something. Just for safety. I'll put you on the insurance." Michael was already forming a new plan to save his dirty weekend, as he eagerly took down Natalia's details. The meeting went on, with all of them quite unaware of the tiny camera in a dark corner of the room.

****

In another city, a short man in a suit nodded his head, and clicked off the screen. "Exactly as we'd planned," he said.

"Of course," said the figure beside him. "How could it not be?"

Bernie

Helen did her best to look cheerful as her companions assembled outside the student union. Other than the sheeting rain, the only sounds to be heard were Bernie's rendition of *Club Tropicana*, and Mycroft lecturing the four dancers about Union rules concerning joint events between societies. One of the new walking club members was a thin, bespectacled young man in a battered coat, who'd given his name as Martin, then fallen silent. The other hadn't spoken at all, but he was unmistakeable with jet black skin, perfect in its smoothness, and a gentle face. He looked like he'd been dressed by his grandmother, in a big-collared pale shirt and a chunky jumper, the nerdy outfit somehow utterly at odds with his skin tone. Helen wondered what his story was, but there was no way of knowing, since she'd never yet heard him speak. He'd signed his name as Denny on the sheet.

When Michael arrived with the minibus, everyone rushed to board, desperate to avoid getting any wetter, or having to sit next to Mycroft. Janelle and Lysandra gasped with disdainful amazement when they learned that the side and back doors of the minibus didn't open, meaning they had to join members of the Wacky Walkers in climbing their way backwards from the front passenger seats.

"You'd better stay in the front, Natalia," said Michael. "I can show you the controls on the bus."

Natalia slotted in beside him and watched intently as he showed her the controls, one by one, while he looked at her legs with similar concentration. It reminded him of how he would be spending the weekend. "And which one is choke?" she asked.

"There's no choke."

"Then how it start?"

"It starts without choke."

"I no understand."

Michael started and restarted the bus three times. "See? No need for choke."

Natalia gave a worried nod. Helen slipped into the third seat at the front. "You guys going to be dancing as soon as you arrive?"

"Just fun dance tonight. We have big demonstration dance tomorrow. Much practise. Every day."

Michael felt a twinge of guilt. But these girls wouldn't be going anywhere without his club, he reminded himself. He looked again at Natalia's legs, and fingered the strawberry in his pocket. With the passengers all loaded up and the spaces between seats packed with rucksacks, he pulled the bus to the car park exit. There, he found the way blocked by two arguing cyclists and their prone, entangled bicycles.

"Get out the fucking way!" Michael yelled. The two cyclists both stopped and looked at him with curious expressions, then resumed their argument. "I don't care whose fucking fault it was," shouted Michael, "but if you don't shift arse this minute I will personally flatten your fucking bikes!"

"I no think that will be good for minibus," said Natalia.

Then, quite suddenly, one of the cyclists glanced at his watch, and they both picked up their bikes and walked away. "Arseholes!" yelled Michael as he pulled the bus, at last, onto the road. The windscreen wipers were already going at full speed, and an oily smell filled the bus as the heating system gasped out tepid air from the dashboard. A few minutes passed, and then Michael rubbed his head and gave a little groan.

Helen

"You OK?" said Helen.

"Had a headache all day," he lied. "It's nothing."

"Many people die with meningitis," said Natalia. "Always first say is only headache."

Michael smiled. This girl was a godsend! Behind him Mycroft was earnestly describing to Lysandra some recent changes to traffic regulations, while Bernie was attempting to start a singsong.

"'Ere, stick this on," grunted Lucy from behind him, handing forward a CD.

Helen tried, but the minibus sound system proved to be utterly dead. She handed the *Frozen* soundtrack back to Lucy. "Waste of fuckin' time bringin' it," muttered Lucy.

Ten minutes later, Michael surreptitiously pulled a strawberry from his pocket and slipped it into his mouth. Most people would regard a strawberry allergy as an annoyance, but Michael believed that from adversity came opportunity. Soon after that, as they made their way out of the city, the disquiet in his body began to build outwards from his stomach.

*****

The two cyclists arrived at the door of their flat. "How the hell did he know that minibus would come at exactly that moment?" asked one.

"Dunno," said the other. "Easiest hundred quid I've ever earned though."

"But why would anyone want us to hold up a minibus for exactly two minutes and forty-one seconds?" pondered the first.

In the middle of the minibus, Dylan was assessing his options. Lucy scared him. If by some miracle he got a date with her, he'd probably spend it hiding under the table. She was meant for one far bolder than he.

Natalia, he thought, was much more shaggable. Round face, big soulful eyes, and well supplied in the breast department. However, he'd noticed the way that Martin, one of the two new recruits, had been gazing at her since he'd taken the seat behind her. As if divine light radiated from the back of her head. Although he suspected that Martin might be even more inept with girls than he was, Dylan did not want to intercede, having experienced for himself that kind of hopelessly intense longing.

Janelle had long pale brown hair that a more critical eye than Dylan's might have called lank. From Dylan's simpler perspective, she had nice eyes, nice lips and a pulse. However she also had a silver crucifix hanging on a chain around her neck, which would probably mean too much church and too little sex. There was a certain solemnity about her, too.

This left Lysandra. She was tall and thin, with a skin tone that suggested mixed ancestry, and her jet black curly hair reached her shoulder. Face pretty, but in an unusual way; she looked frighteningly intelligent. But she'd do. Yes, she'd definitely do. It helped a lot that she was squashed in beside him, and trying to extract herself from being talked at by Mycroft. Even so, it took five minutes for Dylan to think of something to say:

"Hello."

"Hello," she said back.

"I'm Dylan."

"Lysandra."

"That's an unusual name."

"It's Greek, I think. My mum's into ancient history."

"It is indeed of Greek origin," said Mycroft. "Lysandra was a Macedonian queen, married to Alexander the fifth. The name means 'one who brings freedom'. Although in her case, 'one who repeatedly marries powerful cousins' would have been more apt."

"Thank you for that," said Lysandra.

"I think it's a nice name," said Dylan.

"Thanks. That's a really sweet thing to say."

"Dylan, on the other hand, comes from the Welsh for 'intensive flow'," said Mycroft.

Janelle

*****

The minibus now moved onto a slip road, and a sign announced that they were joining the M6. "We go on motorway?" asked Natalia, worriedly.

"Of course," said Helen. "Otherwise it would take all night."

"You no say we go on motorway. I never drive on motorway. In home always little roads."

"Well, don't worry," said Helen. "You won't have to drive unless it's an emergency."

"Quite," said Michael, as his skin started to get hotter. He tried not to think about what Natalia had just said.

Fifteen miles further on, Michael was clearly unwell. The traffic was heavy and made slower by the sheeting rain, so they hadn't got as far as he'd expected. It was another ten miles to the services. He was beginning to shiver. That had never happened before. Then a voluminous fart erupted from beneath him, forcing Helen to wind down her window and get splattered with rain. Natalia held her nose and looked at him. "I think you are ill. You must stop driving."

"I'm fine," he croaked.

"Traffic regulations state..." began Mycroft.

"Shut up!" said Helen. "Michael, I think you need to pull over. You're shaking."

"I'm fine. I can make it to the services, then we'll see," he said.

As he spoke there was a rumbling sound as the bus strayed onto the hard shoulder.

"I'm not asking, I'm telling. Stop the bus right now," shouted Helen, and she reached over to hit the hazard lights. Michael, his head starting to spin, had no choice but to obey. He didn't understand it. His last reaction, two years ago, had been nothing like this. There'd been an impressive rash and a temperature, but nothing more, and it had been gone inside three hours. But those had been cooked strawberries, he suddenly realised. He managed to stop the bus, and another resounding fart issued forth. Some of the others piled out of the bus onto the verge, like Helen preferring the rain to the smell. Mycroft dutifully placed the red triangle exactly 45 metres behind the bus (he paced them out). Meanwhile Lysandra, who was a medical student, examined Michael and pronounced herself stumped. Helen and Lucy had a quick conference and agreed to call an ambulance and have it meet them at the services.

Natalia was bundled into the driving seat, and Michael into the back, after which everyone had to wait for ycroft to retrieve the red warning triangle. Lucy jumped into the front passenger seat with Helen.

"How you make it start?" asked Natalia.

"Just pretend I'm holding the choke," said Helen. "See, I'm pulling it now."

The engine roared into life, and the bus lurched as the engine fought the handbrake. Natalia searched on her right le for a handbrake to disengage, while Helen eventually did it for her. The bus jumped forward, and a horn blared t as a car shot past in the next lane.

"I can go in lane now? Is okay?" asked Natalia. The minibus puttered along the hard shoulder at walking speed. ore cars whizzed past. A rumbling sound as the bus strayed towards the slow lane. More angry horns. Natalia ed to change gear and stalled.

"Maybe I should drive," said Helen. "I've not passed yet but this is an emergency!"

"I regret to inform you that if you did, I would be forced to effect a citizen's arrest," said Mycroft.

"Try it," snarled Lucy, "and I'll effect this handbrake right up your – "

"Indicate right!" shouted Helen, as Natalia restarted the engine. "Now watch in the mirror!" A few moments ssed. Helen craned round to see in the mirror herself. "Yes pull out now!" The bus lumbered into the slow lane. or a minute or so they tootled along at ten miles per hour. Then a mass of traffic began passing them in the middle ne, and a pair of headlights appeared close behind them. The hooting started again.

"I have to go faster?" asked Natalia.

"A little faster, yes," said Helen. To her surprise, Natalia now seemed to have grasped how to change gears and celerate. Gradually their speed picked up, until miraculously they were zooming along at the same speed as eryone else. Natalia sat hunched forward, her eyes locked on the road ahead, her right leg jiggling under her skirt. ney were coming up fast upon a lorry in the slow lane.

"And now I am taking-over, yes?" Natalia said joyfully, and pulled the bus into the middle lane without waiting r an answer. Helen winced as tyres screeched behind them. Yet more angry horns.

"S-services!" said Michael from behind them. Helen saw the big blue sign as they moved in front of the lorry. it there was another lorry ahead of it.

"I should go there?" asked Natalia, pointing at the exit looming ahead.

"Slow down a bit," said Helen. "NOT LIKE THAT" she shrieked, as Natalia pushed down hard on the brake, rcing everyone forward in their seats. The lorries moved ahead once more, but there were cars behind them now.

"Now I move big arrow lever?" said Natalia, meaning the left-indicator.

Helen thought fast. "No, stay in this lane! We'll have to get the next services." The exit flew by. Behind her, a ivering Michael thought miserably of his car, sitting in the services car park, where he'd left it earlier that day, fore hitching back. The service station had an on-site first aider, and his plan had been to be left with him while atalia drove everyone else on to Glasgow. Michael would have en driven back to collect Suzy as soon as he felt well enough. nd he'd planned it so well!

"Call the ambulance again," said Helen.

"No signal," said Lucy.

Helen noticed some flashing lights far behind them. ammit, that must be the ambulance coming already. talia, when you can, please move into the left lane and y there. Once we get a signal we can pull over."

Natalia glanced to the left and turned the wheel.

"No wait!" screamed Lucy.

From nowhere, a car had caught up with them in the slow e, doing well over 100. It swerved as the bus lurched into t lane, then the speeding car was searing up the sloping ge ahead of them, still at a ridiculous speed. For a ment Helen thought it would reach the top and take flight. tead, it suddenly started to roll, tumbling as it rocketed wards, but there was a bridge ahead and –

The explosion shook the minibus, flames shooting out m the wrecked car ahead of them. Natalia seemed to ve frozen, and they were heading straight for it.

Natalia

.***.

Barry Walton's life was flashing before his eyes. He felt himself hanging in the middle of some kind of theatre, above all the empty seats, while scenes from his life unfolded in front of him on a giant screen. Barry found the whole thing strangely unconcerning, although the little red guy in the bottom right corner taking notes had been a bit of a surprise. At one point, when a nine-year-old Barry added dog shit to the lunch box of a much larger boy who'd been bullying him, the little red man grinned at him and gave him a few theatrical claps. Barry also saw his own father, now long dead, hitting both him and his mother. Again the little red man caught his eye, this time pointing first to his father, and then downwards, in a gesture that Barry instinctively understood. Perhaps he'd be meeting his father again very soon.

As time moved forward, he saw himself turning into his father: drinking, slapping girlfriends, starting fights. Occasionally, when his opponents fought back, the little red man would swing his fists in encouragement. With every strike, and every cruel word Barry uttered, the little red man typed, and a red column on the right side of the screen grew a little bit higher. Then he saw himself suddenly in a hospital, by the bedside of the mother who'd run out on him when he was eleven, taking his baby sister with her. She told him she was dying. Barry watched his former self telling her that he forgave her, even though he'd known he couldn't. He'd wondered then if she believed him, and seeing it again now, he wondered still. She smiled anyway. A little blue man with wings appeared in the bottom left corner of his screen, looking surprised to be there. After a moment searching his pocket, he drew out a device like the one the red man had, hit a few buttons, and a blue column appeared. It was totally dwarfed by the red one. The watching Barry looked on miserably. Was that really the first good thing he had done in his life?

Barry realised, now, the cruel irony of it: how that one good thing would lead to his end. He'd come to see his mother almost every day after that, missing only the days when he had to sign on. The little blue column crept up slowly. After a week, he'd gone in and found his mother not alone. A little boy had been with her, and a young woman. Emmie, Barry's sister. The sister he'd once promised to protect, before his father's fists had showed him that he couldn't. That day with Emmie and the boy had also been the very last time he'd seen his mother; he hadn't known it then, and because he'd been overcome with shock at seeing his sister, he'd barely even said goodbye to his mother. The watching Barry wanted to cry, but he couldn't.

Next he saw himself with his sister, standing together at their mother's funeral, promising to look after each other as the little boy wept between them. For Barry, it had turned out, this meant picking fights with whatever man his sister was going out with at the time, because Barry could see in them the things he hated in himself. Some he sent packing, others dared him to hit them in front of Emmie. When he wasn't battling them, he was having shouting matches with Emmie over whether he should be minding his own business. Had his whole life been one big argument? Even the red and blue men were arguing now, each trying to claim these crude attempts at chivalry for their own column. Watching them, Barry felt himself smiling for what he knew might be the last ever time. Let them squabble, he didn't care. What else did he ever have to offer his sister? Then the screen showed the time when he'd got wind of someone bullying little Austin, his nephew. Barry had tracked the boy down, and made sure he wouldn't be hurting Austin again anytime soon. That went firmly into the red column.

When Austin's eighth birthday approached, Barry had been able to afford nothing more than a few tatty toys from a charity shop. Then, coming home from the pub, he'd seen a magnificent kid's bike, sitting by the front gate of a big garden. '*What kind of mum lets kids leave valuable things where they could get nicked?*' he'd thought. '*One who can afford to replace them, that's who.*' The red column grew again. Austin had loved his new bike. But two weeks later the original owners had somehow found out, and claimed their bike back. Barry then saw himself sitting in his dusty mess of a flat, hearing his sister scream abuse at him down the phone. When at last she'd gone silent, he'd muttered that he would make it right.

He'd found the same model for sale in a shop. So expensive. He'd accepted a loan from Sonny Money. Paid for the bike with the wad of cash. Saw Austin's delighted face when he got his bike again, accepted a hug from his sister. The red man clicked his fingers, reviving the blue man, who'd apparently fallen asleep. The blue column rose again, but still it was so far behind.

A month of trying and failing to get money. Sonny Money's toothy grin as he gave his ultimatum, mentioning how sweet he thought little Austin was. Acting like some Vegas crimelord, as if his many visible fillings were gold not crumbling grey amalgam. Barry had borrowed the gun from Mad Gordie, thought about using it on Sonny, but he knew the guy had friends. He'd opted for robbery instead. The final act.

Barry watched himself walk into that corner shop. Saw how his hand shook like crazy as he pointed the gun at the shop assistant. Heard himself telling the man he had nothing to lose, and the man readily believed him. Then that terrifying voice from behind him:

"Barry Walton!"

The screen showed it all in slow motion, just like a movie. Barry saw himself spin round, heart pounding, eyes locking with the fearful visage of Mister Howarth, his English teacher from long ago. Greyer hair, but those same piercing eyes. Muscles clenched all over Barry's body. Including his trigger finger. Mister Howarth's chest exploded into a mass of blood. For a moment he stood still, as if ready to prove school rumours that Howarth really was a Lord of the Undead. Then Howarth spoke, in a whisper. You knew it was big trouble when Mister Howarth spoke softly. "You stupid, little, … uuuhhhhh." Then he fell to the ground stone dead. Barry turned round to the shop assistant, but the man had disappeared off somewhere.

"I didn't mean to!" Barry cried, to anyone who could hear him. "That man scares the hell out of me, always has! I didn't mean to!!" Then he turned and fled. The little red man pulled a lever, and the blue one fell through a trapdoor. The red man waved him goodbye, as the red column swelled to fill half of the screen, and started flashing.

Barry was running; sirens were wailing. He saw a man getting out of a car, grabbed him and threw him over, took the keys and drove off. The red man cheered. Barry's new car screeched through the city, gunning red lights, flattening a fox. The red man was now eating popcorn, sitting back and enjoying the ride. No need to take notes anymore. Barry made it onto the motorway. Rain was sheeting down, and Barry loved that. Again the watching Barry experienced that strange mixture of despair and elation he'd felt at the time, as he'd screamed through the traffic, faster and faster. Despair, because he'd known that within minutes – hours at the most, he'd be dead or locked up. Elation, because that meant that nothing mattered. He was finally free. He reached the motorway with the police close behind him, but they couldn't get ahead without causing an accident themselves. Hah! Advantage Barry. But all those idiots in the fast lane doing only 80 were blocking his way. He cut through the middle lane into the slow lane, slammed his foot down even harder, zoomed past the middle lane slowcoaches. Then one of them switched lanes suddenly, right in front of him. An ugly yellow minibus. There was nowhere to go except the verge, but he lost control, thundering through the grass up the embankment, until the front wheel hit something and the car took off, spinning. The concrete of a motorway bridge rushed to greet him.

.**.

Back in the corner shop, William Howarth blinked as the recording of his own life came to an end. The memory of it faded fast, like a dream. He was pleasantly surprised to see an Angel appear inside the shop, along with a shining blue stairway, and a strangely familiar guitar chord.

"Does that music play for everyone?"

"Only Led Zep fans," smiled the Angel.

"I wasn't sure where I'd go, you know. I spent most of my life terrifying children."

"Perhaps they needed it," replied the Angel.

"Could I ask that … could I hang on a few minutes? Only I was supposed to meet my daughter here, and I haven't seen her in three years. Would be nice to see her, one last time."

The Angel looked puzzled. "Your daughter is still in Australia."

"But she called … it was a local number," said Howarth.

"Wasn't her," said the Angel. "It was someone pretending."

"But why?" asked Howarth, looking down at his own dead body. "Why would someone do that?"

"That's not my concern," said the Angel. "Nor yours, anymore."

.***.

Helen grabbed the minibus steering wheel and forced them first into the middle lane, then to the fast lane, while other vehicles braked hard and dropped behind them. The fire and smoke from the crashed car came closer and closer, then in a moment it whipped past.

"Bad thing happening," said Natalia.

"Well we just pretty much killed someone, so yeah, you could say," snarled Lucy.

"Visions come back. Very bad. Babushka have them many times. I, also. See people who are gone. Very bad!"

"Natalia, please, you're in shock. Just pull us over to the slow lane, we need to stop the bus!"

"I should leave this road?"

"We need to stop," said Helen. "Pull over!"

"But there is car!" Natalia complained.

Lucy glanced at the empty slow lane. "There's nothing! Pull over."

Natalia decided she must have failed to understand how mirrors worked. Maybe the reflection she saw was her own vehicle? If she didn't pull over now she'd miss another turning. The exit was clearly marked ahead, and there was even a man standing there, beckoning with his arms, grinning. Perhaps he was with the ambulance? Natalia pulled the bus across into the slow lane and indicated left for the exit. The white car in the wing mirror veered onto the verge, its brakes screeching. Natalia steered towards the exit, but now the man was running into the road, waving his arms like crazy, looking horrified. His face, in fact all of him, was a bright shade of red. He seemed to have horns, too. And a tail. Natalia tried to steer around him, but the wheel had locked. Their eyes locked, too. His were yellow, with blazing red pupils, and below them the mouth had razor-sharp fangs, which would have been terrifying if the whole red face were not now bearing an expression of total panic. She waved back at the man, "Go way go way go way!!!" But the man didn't move.

There were three bumps – front bumper, front wheels and back wheels. Everyone felt them.

"What the fuck was that?" said Lucy

Natalia watched the prone red figure in the rear view mirror recede. She said nothing.

"Where did the motorway go?" asked Helen. "Where are we?"

The road they were on had only one lane, and it was going steadily downhill …

To be continued … Kindle £1.99 or Paperback £6.66

Printed in Great Britain
by Amazon

72193049R00047